To Michèle

Groundwood Books / House of Anansi Press
110 Spadina Avenue, Suite 801
Toronto, Ontario, Canada M5V 2K4
Distributed in the U.S.A. by Publishers Group West
1700 Fourth Street, Berkeley, CA 94710

We acknowledge for their financial support of our publishing program the Canada Council
for the Arts, the Government of Canada through the Book Publishing Industry
Development Program (BPIDP) and the Ontario Arts Council.

ONTARIO ARTS COUNCIL
CONSEIL DES ARTS DE L'ONTARIO

Library and Archives Canada Cataloguing in Publication
Gay, Marie-Louise
Good Morning Sam / Marie-Louise Gay
ISBN 0-88899-528-8 (bound).– 0-88899-678-0 (pbk.)
I. Title.
PS8563.A868G66 2003   jC813'.54   C2002-902935-X
PZ7

Library of Congress Control Number: 2002108235
Printed and bound in China

GOOD MORNING
SAM

MARIE-LOUISE GAY

A GROUNDWOOD BOOK   HOUSE OF ANANSI PRESS   TORONTO   BERKELEY

"Sam," called Stella. "Wake up!"

"I'm awake," yawned Sam. "I think."

"I'll help you get dressed," said Stella.
"No," said Sam. "I can do it by myself."

"Are you sure?"
"Yes," said Sam.

"Hurry up, then," said Stella.

"I'm hurrying," said Sam.

"Stella, help!" called Sam.
"My head grew bigger in the night."

"No, it didn't," said Stella.
"Ouf!" said Sam.

"Stella!" called Sam. "I can't find my underpants."
"Did you look in the bottom drawer?" asked Stella.
"I'm looking," said Sam.

"Sam," said Stella. "Are you in there?"
"Yes," answered Sam.

"Stella, help!" called Sam.
"I can't see. Did you turn off the lights?"

"No, I didn't," said Stella. "See?"
"Ouf!" said Sam.

"Stella! My sock has disappeared!"

"No, it didn't," said Stella. "Here it comes."

"Stella! Now my shoes are lost!
"Have you looked everywhere, Sam?"

"Yes," said Sam.
"Did you look in the closet?" asked Stella.

"Help!" cried Sam. "I can't get out."

"Sam? Are you in there?"
"No," said Sam.

"Stella, I'm ready! And I did it all by myself!"

"Didn't you forget something, Sam?"
"Oh," said Sam. "My pants!"

"Ta-daa!" sang Sam. "I'm really ready now."
"Finally," said Stella. "Let's go."

"Stella?" said Sam.
"What now?" sighed Stella.

"Didn't you forget something?" giggled Sam.